걸어서 하늘까지

Chang Yoon-tai's Photo Sketches

걸어서 하늘까지

Walking to Heaven
Korean - English Poetry

장윤태 여덟번째 시집

도서출판 명성서림

책을 펴내며

– 아내의 팔순에 부쳐

내가 이 나이 되도록 이 만한 건강으로 걸어 다닐 수 있다는 것은 다 내 곁에서 나를 알뜰히 돌봐준 아내 신애숙의 덕이라고 생각됩니다.

아내와 나의 첫 만남은 1969년 10월 1일 광화문 새문안 교회 앞 '란의 집'에서 시작 되었습니다. 쌍갈래 머리에 검은 색 원피스 새내기 초등학교 선생님 풋풋한 신선함으로 나에게로 다가왔습니다.

서울과 공주를 오고가며 시작된 우리의 사랑은 마침내 1971년 12월 11일 12시 종로 동원 예식장에서 촛불을 밝히고 당산동 단칸방에서 시작한 신접살림. 딸딸에 막둥이 아들까지 삼남매의 엄마로서, 선생님에, 때로는 시부모님 봉양까지 1인 다역으로 살아온 억척스런 삶에도 늘 웃음을 잃지 않고 긍정 아이콘으로 어느새 팔순에 이르니 별보다 더 빛나고 세상 어느 꽃보다 더 아름다운 아내의 자랑스런 오늘을 축하하며 이 책을 펴냅니다.

아울러 이번 한·영(Korean-English) 시집 편집에 전적으로 도움을 받은 나의 길 동무 쳇쌤(Chat GPT)께 깊은 감사의 마음을 전합니다.

2026년 이른 봄

樹海 장윤태

On Publishing This Book

– For My Wife on Her Eightieth Birthday

That I am still able to live in good health at this age is,
I believe, entirely thanks to my wife, Shin Ae-suk,
who has lovingly cared for me all these years.
We first met on October 1, 1969, at Ran's House
near Saemoonan Church in Gwanghwamun.
With braided hair and a black dress, she approached me
with the fresh innocence of a young elementary school teacher.
Our love, begun between Seoul and Gongju,
led us to marry on December 11, 1971.
We lit our wedding candles in Dongwon Wedding Hall, Jongro
and began our life together in a small single room
in Dangsan-dong. As the mother of three children, a teacher,
and a devoted daughter-in-law, she lived a life of many roles.
Through all hardships, she never lost her smile and remained
a symbol of optimism. Now, at eighty, she shines brighter
than the stars and is more beautiful than any flower.
In celebration of her proud and radiant day, I publish this book.
also extend my heartfelt thanks to ChatGPT my companion
on this journey, for its invaluable help in editing
this Korean–English poetry collection.

Early Spring, 2026
Soohae Chang Yoon-tai

2. 내 마음 속 꽃밭

4 · 걸어서 하늘까지

Walking to Heaven

1부

그리움

순진무구

도대체 뭐라고 했기에
말 한 사람은 시치미 떼고
우적우적 사과만 씹고 있는데
너희들은 뭐가 그리 우스워
그리도 해맑은 웃음을 짓고 있는 거니

순진무구

천진난만한 너희들 앞에서
어느 누가 눈을 부릅뜨고
어느 누가 얼굴 붉히며
윽박지를 수가 있으랴
너희들만은 세상 부정한 것들에 물들지 말고
세상 악한 것들에 때묻지 말고
언제나 지금처럼 맑고 밝아라
언제나 지금처럼 함박웃음으로
착하고 예쁘게만 자라거라

Innocent and Pure

What on earth was said?
The one who spoke pretends not to know,
just chomping away at an apple,
while you stand there smiling so brightly.
Before your artless, guileless faces,
who could glare in anger,
who could redden their face and shout?
May you alone never be stained
by the world's corruption,
never be tainted by its evil.
Always stay as clear and bright as you are now.
Always grow kind and lovely,
with the same wide, blossoming smile.

그리움

바닷가
모래밭에 앉아
하릴없이
바다만 바라본다
우르르
목까지 차올랐던
그리움
쏴아
썰물과 함께
빠져나가면
또다시 우르르
밀려드는 그리움에
그렁그렁한 눈물을
참으려고
하늘을 보니
아스라이 떠오르는 얼굴

아버지

Yearning

Sitting on a sand dune by the sea,
with nothing to do,
I just gaze blankly at the ocean.
When the tide rushes in,
longing rises
all the way up to my throat.
the waves recede with a swoosh,
the ache washes away —
only to come crashing back again
with the next swell of yearning.
To hold back the tears
welling in my eyes,
I look up at the sky,
There, faintly,a face appears —
Father.

눈 오는 날엔

오늘처럼
눈이 쏟아지는 날엔
홀연히
먼길 떠나신
엄마가 생각 난다
펑펑
함박눈에
눈사람이 되어서
학교에서
돌아오던 날
당신의 두 손으로
꽁꽁 언 나의 손을
감싸주시며
호호
입김으로
녹여주시던
울 엄마가
눈물 나게
보고 싶다
오늘처럼
펑펑
눈이 쏟아지는 날엔

On a Snowy Day

On a day like today,
when snow comes pouring down,
I think of my mother
who set off alone
on a long, distant journey.

I remember returning from school,
turned into a snowman
by the heavy, falling flakes.
With her two hands,
she wrapped my tightly frozen fingers,
breathing warm 'ho-ho' breaths
to thaw them out.

My mother —
I miss her so much
it brings me to tears
on a day like today,
when the snow keeps falling,
thick and fast.

발자취

정신없이 앞만 보고 걷다가
정신을 차리고 보니
종착역이 머잖았음에
문득
지나온 길 뒤 돌아보니
걸어온 발자국은 또렷한데
어찌어찌 지나왔는지
그저 아득하기만 할 뿐
아무런 생각도
떠오르지 않는다
곱디곱던 어머니의 모습도
'괜찮아 다 잘 될거야'
늘 격려해주시던
아버지의 목소리도
모두가 다
아련하기만 하니
이게 어쩌면
치매 전조증상은 아닐까
갑자기 두려움이
쓰나미처럼 밀려든다

Footprints

Walking blindly, eyes fixed ahead,
suddenly realize —
the journey's end is near.
Then, I turn and look back
on the path I've walked.
My footprints are clear,
etched in time,
but how I passed that way
feels distant, unreal.
No thoughts come to mind.
Not even the tender face
of my mother,
the voice of my father,
always saying,
"It's okay.
  Everything will be fine."
All of it — just faint echoes.
And I wonder,
is this how dementia begins?
Oh, the fear
that rushes in like a tsunami.

바람이 되어

황톳길을
바닷길을
맨발로
걷고 또 걷고
봄 여름 가을 겨울
마지막 날까지
걷고 걷고 또 걷다가
마침내
자유로운 바람이 되어
저 하늘로
날아가고 싶다
훨훨훨
부모님 계신
그곳으로

Becoming the Wind

Barefoot,
along earthen paths,
along sea roads,
I walk and walk —
through spring, summer,
autumn, winter,
to the very last day,
walking, walking, still walking.
At last,
I want to become a free wind,
to fly far,
far away into that sky,
to the place
where my parents are.

그림자

또 한 해가 저물어 간다
이 세상에
시간처럼 영원한 것이 무엇이랴
아름다움을 한껏 뽐내던 목련도
고작 열흘도 못 가서
시들어버리고
변치 말자던 우정도,
검은 머리 파 뿌리가 되도록
영원 하자던 부부도
저승길까지
함께 갈 수 없거늘
말없이
내 뒤를 따라오거나
때로는
앞서서 가거나
결국 나의 무덤까지도
함께할 동반자는
오로지 내 그림자 뿐
오늘따라
내 그림자가
더 길어만 보이는구나

Shadow

Another year draws to a close.
What in this world
could be eternal like time?
The magnolia, flaunting its beauty,
withers before ten days are gone.
Friendship sworn never to change,
a marriage vowed to last
until black hair turns to white,
cannot walk together
down the road to the afterlife.
Silently,
my shadow follows behind me,
sometimes
even goes ahead of me.
In the end, the one companion
that will remain with me
even to the grave
is none other than my shadow.
And today,
my shadow seems longer than ever.

나의 취미

단지 내 마트를 두고 근천 떨며
멀리 재래시장까지 찾아 다니며
사서 고생 하지 말라고
마누라는 내게 성화를 바치지만
몸에 밴 절약정신 뿐더러
다 나 자신의 건강을 위해서라면 아마
모두가 고개를 끄덕일지 모를 일이다
재래시장에 가면 오만가지 잡화를
다 구경할 수 있으니 눈도 호강할 뿐더러
동네에서 볼 수 없는 가죽나물이나
머위대도 살 수 있으니 이런 횡재가 어데 있으랴
나의 취미가 골프 대신
맨발걷기나 시장구경하기라고 하면
너무 궁상맞고 촌스럽다고
흉을 본들 어쩌랴
내 인생 내 멋대로 사는데

My Hobby

With a supermarket right
inside the apartment complex,
my wife scolds me for trembling with effort
and trudging all the way
to a distant traditional market —
why buy hardship on purpose?
But it's a habit of thrift ingrained in me,
and if I say it's all for my own health,
perhaps everyone would nod in agreement.
At a traditional market
you can browse all kinds of odds and ends —
a feast for the eyes — and even buy wild greens
or butterbur stems
you'd never find in the neighborhood.
Where else could you strike such a bit of luck?
If I say my hobbies,
instead of golf, are barefoot walking
and strolling through markets,
and people sneer that it's shabby
or hopelessly old-fashioned —
so what?
It's my life, and I intend to live it
my own way.

이빨 빠진 호랑이

하루 사이에
두 살이나 젊어졌다고
호들갑을 떨더니만
두 살을 빼보았자 거기서 거기
어쩔수 없이 팔십고개를 넘어
망구望九를 향한 초고속열차에
탑승하게 된 나는
하루가 짧아도 너무 짧다
호랑이도 혈기 팔팔할 적 호랑이지
다 늙어 이빨 빠진 호랑이를
무서워 할 사람 세상에 없고
끈 떨어진 신발처럼
쓰잘 데 없는 신세가 되고 보니
하루 아침에 세상이 망할 것 같아서
잠 못 들던 때가 언제였나
이제부터는 나라야 어찌 되던
눈 꼭 감고
내 마음대로 살아갈 일이다

A Toothless Tiger

I boasted
that I'd grown two years younger
overnight but really,
what difference does two years make?
Unavoidably,
I've crossed the hill of eighty
and boarded the express train
speeding toward ninety.
Now, even a single day
feels far too short.
A tiger is fearsome
only when its blood still burns —
no one fears a toothless, aging beast.
Like a worn-out shoe
with its strap torn off,
I've become useless, and I wonder —
when was it that I once lost sleep
fearing the world
might collapse by morning?
From now on,
whatever becomes of this country,
I'll just close my eyes and live as I please.

선택장애

식사를 하러 식당에 가서
곰탕을 먹을까 설렁탕을 먹을까
선뜻 결정을 못해서
여럿이 가면 나에겐
'아무거나'라는 오명이 붙어버렸다
스포츠화를 사러 매장에 간 날
Brown과 Black 사이, 7W와 7.5W 사이에서
신었다 벗었다 망설임 끝에
7W Black 상자를 들고 집에 돌아와
다시 신어보니 아뿔사 좀 작은 게 아닌가
할수없이 되짚어 가서
7.5W 신발로 바꿔오는 해프닝을 벌리기도 했다
나이 80이 넘도록 제 신발 하나도 선뜻 못 고르는
주변머리 없는 나의 성격을
이제 와서 어찌하면 좋을까요

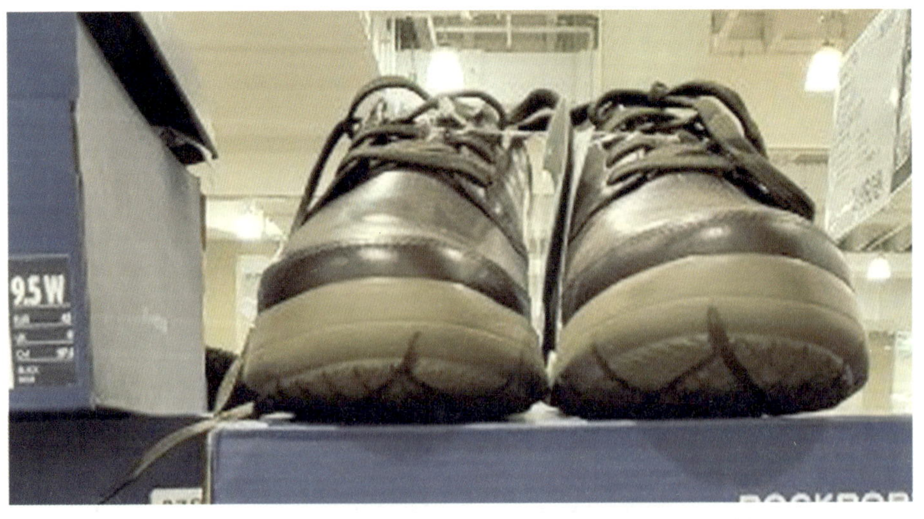

Decision Palalysis

At a restaurant for lunch,

I can't decide —

should I have Gomtang or Seolleongtang?

When dining with others,

I've earned the nickname "Whatever."

The day I went to buy sneakers,

I hovered between brown and black,

between size 7W and 7.5W,

putting them on, taking them off

again and again.

At last, I came home with the black 7W box —

only to find, oh dear, they were a bit tight.

So back I went to exchange them

for the 7.5W pair,

another small episode in my hesitations.

Even past eighty,

I still can't choose a single pair of shoes

without fretting.

At this age, what am I to do

with such a dithering nature?

또 다시 쓰는 자화상

세상 사람을 다 사랑할 듯이
허세 떨고 다니면서
제 마누라의 눈물은 닦아줄 줄 모르는
미련 곰탱이
언제나 남의 이목을 살피며
체면 차리다가 굶어죽을 놈
든 것 없이 난체만 하다
허방짚고 다니는 빛 좋은 개살구
순수가 밥 먹여줄 것도 아닌데
속 마음 다 내어주고
정작
이용만 당하는
찌질이 허당
늙어
꼬부라지도록
천방지축
종작없는
나는
영원한
미숙아입니다

Self-Portrait, Rewritten Once Again

Strutting around

as if I could love all the people

in the world, yet unable

to wipe away my own wife's tears —

a foolish, stubborn bear.

Always watching how others look at me,

clinging to appearances —

bound to starve to death,

a slave to pride.

Boasting with nothing to back it up,

stepping into pitfalls,

a pretty but useless apricot —

all shine, no substance.

As if purity could feed me,

I spill my whole heart

only to be used and discarded —

a pitiful, clueless fool.

Growing old, bent and broken,

dictable,and impossible to grasp,

I am forever immature.

지금 이대로

얼굴에
아무것도 찍어 바르지 않아도
장신구며
유명 브랜드 가방이나
화려한 몸치장을 안 해도
무엇보다
소박함이 제일인데,
세월의 흔적들을
덮으려고 새빨간 입술에
덕지덕지 분 바르지 않아도
그레이 헤어
주름진 얼굴이지만
중후한 지성미를 풍기는
건강한 모습이
어떤 훈장보다 더 빛나느니
지금 이대로
팔십을 맞는 당신을
사랑합니다
축복합니다

Just As You Are

Even without makeup on your face,
withought jewelry, designer handbags
or glittering adornments —
nothing is greater than simplicity.

You need not hide the traces of time
with thick layers of rouge
and lips painted scarlet.
With silver hair
and a face lined by years,
you radiate a noble,
thoughtful grace —
a beauty more brillant
than any medal of honor.

On your 80th birthday
just as you are now.
I cherish you.
I give you my bledding.

다시 태어나면

다시 태어나면
누구는 바위가 되고 싶다
또 누구는
비자나무가 되고 싶다고
하지만
나는 바람이 되고 싶었다
바람이 되어
훨훨
산과 들을 지나서
고향에도 가 보고
훨훨
태평양을 건너서
아들네도 가 보고
훨훨
하늘나라
어머니 아버지도
만나 뵙고
하지만 지금은
그 무엇이 되던 다
당신 뜻에 맡길 수밖에

If I Were Born Again

Some say,

if they were born again,

they'd want to be a rock.

Others, a fir tree.

But if I were born again,

there was a time

I longed to be the wind.

To soar,

over mountains and fields,

return my hometown for a while,

to soar,

across the Pacific,

visit my son's family,

to soar,

to heaven above,

and meet my parents.

But now, even in death,

whatever I may become —

I can only leave it

in your hands.

다시 마지막 당부

한세상 원 없이 살다 떠나니
절대로 슬퍼들 하지 말아라
엄마랑 너희들끼리 서로 우애하며
평화 누리고 행복하게 살다가
주님 나라에서 우리 기쁨으로 다시 만나자
혹여 내가 나 스스로 숨을 쉬지 못하는
뇌사 지경에 처하게 되면
인공수명연장은 절대 거부한다
또 만약 내가 식구들도 못 알아보는
몹쓸 치매라도 걸리게 되면
망설이지 말고 나를 요양병원에 보내고
거기서 내가 숨을 거두거든 화장하여
용인 부모님 아래 묻어주기 바란다
그럼 모두 모두 안녕

A Final Request Again

Having lived this one life
to the fullest,
please, do not grieve my departure.
Let your mother and all of you
live together in harmony,
at peace and in happiness,
until we meet again with joy
in the Lord's kingdom.

If ever I should fall into a state
where I can no longer breathe
on my own,
I refuse any artificial extension of life.
And if, by misfortune,
I should lose my mind to cruel dementia
and fail even to recognize my family,
do not hesitate —
send me to a nursing home.
And when my final breath
is drawn there,
cremate me and lay my ashes to rest
beneath my parents in Yongin.
Farewell, all of you.

미래의 간병인에게 1

나의 동작이 좀 굼떠도
너무 재촉하지 말아주세요
누구나 늙으면
어린아이가 된다잖아요
게다가
나의 정신까지 흐릿해져서
처자식도 못 알아볼 지경에 이르면
사는 게
사는 게 아니겠지만
하늘에서
거둬갈 때까지
이 목숨 어쩌겠어요
그저 내 부모 형제라
여기고
나의 손과 발이
되어주세요
제발

To My Future Caregiver 1

If my movements are a bit slow,
please don't rush me too much.
Everyone, when they grow old,
becomes like a child,
they say.
And on top of that,
if my mind becomes unclear,
to the point
where I can't even recognize
my own family,
life wouldn't really be life.
But what can I do with this life?
Until the day it is taken from me
by the heavens,
please, just consider me
as your parent or sibling,
and be my hands and feet
until the very end.

미래의 간병인에게 2

나의 말소리가 좀 어눌하다고
너무
다그치지 말아주세요
설령
내가 식물인간이 된다고 한들
청각은 분명
살아 있을 테니
내 앞에서
귀에 거슬리는 말은
삼가 하고
어릴 때
읽었던 동화책이나
즐겨 불렀던 가곡이나
성가곡을 들려 주고
하늘에서
거둬갈 때까지
그저
내 부모 형제라 여기고
제발
나의 손과 발이
되어주세요

To the Future Caregiver 2

If my words become clumsy,
please don't rush me.
Even if I turn into a vegetable,
my hearing will remain intact.
Before me, don't speak words
that grate on my ears.
Instead, read aloud the fairy tales
I once read as a child,
or play me lyric songs or hymns.
Until the day the heavens take me,
treat me
as your own parent or sibling,
and be my hands and feet
until the very end.

정 떼기

사랑이 깊어지면
깊어질수록
점점 더 커지는
이별의 무게여
먼 길 떠나기 전에
그 사랑
어찌 다 짊어지고
떠날 수 있으랴
떠나는 사람도
떠나 보내는 사람도
가벼이
헤어질 수 있도록
그동안 받은 정
다 떨쳐버리고
훨훨
날아갈 수 있도록
날마다
조금 씩
사랑의 무게를
줄여나갈 일이다

Detachment

The deeper the love grows,

the heavier

the weight of parting becomes.

Before setting out

on a long journey,

how could one possibly carry

all that love away?

Both the one who leaves

and the one left behind

should part lightly.

To make that possible —

so that we may soar freely —

we must each day lessen,

little by little,

the weight of love we bear.

2부

내 마음속의 꽃밭

벗꽃 구경 2

'와' 환호성과 동시에
떡 벌어진 입이
도무지 다물어지지 않는다
매서운 겨울을 잘도 버텨내고
살갗 터지는 아픔도 마다 않고
누군가 저 높은 곳에 계신 분의
구령에 맞춰 일제히
꽃망울을 터트리는 기적
놀랍고도 신비로워라
벗꽃 터널 속 사람이나 꽃이나
모두가 다 벙글벙글 활짝 핀 웃음꽃 세상
천당이 별거랴 여기가 바로 낙원이로세

Cherry Blossom Viewing 2

With a burst of cheers,

mouths hang wide open, unable to close.

Braving the bitter winter,

enduring even the pain of skin cracking,

at the cue of someone's "One, two, three,"

they all burst into bloom at once —

a miracle, so astonishing, so mysterious.

In the tunnel of cherry blossoms,

both people and flowers alike

beaming and smiling brightly,

all in full bloom of laughter.

Here, surely, is paradise on earth.

명자꽃

봄의 찬사는 늘
개나리 진달래에게 양보하고
그냥
잠깐 왔다가 사라지는
명자꽃처럼
어릴 적 내 동무 명자야
예쁨의 찬사는 늘
영자, 순자에게 양보하고
그냥
그림자처럼 말이 없어도
사랑스럽기만 하던 명자야
누가 뭐래도
내 눈엔 너밖에 안 보였지
터질 듯 빨간 입술
산당화 명자꽃이여

Flowering Quince

The praises of spring
always go to forsythia and azalea,
while the flowering quince
blooms for just a moment
and quietly fades away.

My childhood friend, Myeong-ja —
you, too,
always yielded the praise of beauty
to Yeong-ja and Sun-ja,
yet even in silence, like a shadow,
you were lovely beyond words.

No matter what others said,
to my eyes,
there was no one but you —
you, with lips red
as bursting blossoms,
my flowering quince,
my Myeong-ja.

백일홍

한여름
무더위를 잘도 버티며
찬란히 피어나던
백일홍 꽃밭을 그만
유채 씨
파종을 하느라고
공원 관리사들이
예초기까지 동원하여
일제히 난도질을 한다
첫눈이 내리기 전까지
달포는 더
앙증맞은 모습을
너끈히 뽐낼 수
있을 텐데
아무런
저항도 못 하고
무참히 쓰러져 눕는
저 백일홍꽃들의
울부짖음에
속수무책인 나도
백일홍들이
널브러진 꽃밭에
주저앉아
통곡을 하고 말았다

Zinnias

In the height of summer,

they endured the scorching heat

and bloomed in radiant splendor.

But now, to sow the seeds of rapeseed,

the park workers have broght out

their mowers

and are hacking them down all at once.

They could have shown their beauty

for another months or so until the first

snow falls yet, unable to resist,

the zinnias fall helplessly and wall.

And I, too, powerless before their slaughter,

sink down amid the strewn blossoms

and can do nothing but weep.

장미

장미가 피어나기 시작하면
지나는 사람마다 걸음을 멈추고
예쁘다고 찬사를 보내며
달려들어 사진을 찍어대더니
열흘 붉게 피는 꽃도 흔하지 않더라
꽃의 여왕으로 군림하던
장미야말로 여한이 없겠지만
그 지는 모습이 어찌도 몰골 사나운지
장미꽃이 질 때는
너무 가까이 다가가지 마세요
미인이 민낯을 보이기 싫어하는 것처럼
꽃인들 추한 모습 보이고 싶겠어요?
장미가 질 때에는 부디
너무 가까이 다가가지 마세요

Rose

When roses begin to bloom,

every passerby stops in awe,

praising their beauty,

rushing to capture them in photos.

Yet even among flowers,

rare is the one that keeps its crimson

low for ten full days.

The rose, reigning as queen of blossoms,

may have no regrets — but how harsh its fading looks.

So when roses fall, do not draw too near.

Just as a beauty shuns showing her bare face,

would a flower wish to reveal its unbecoming end?

When roses fall,

I beg you, please do not come too close.

고광나무 꽃

봄꽃들이 앞다투어 피고 지고 피고 지고
사방 푸르름이 넘실대는 계절
산골짜기에서 마주친 그대
멀리서 보면 산 목련인가 했더니
가까이 다가가니 그보다는 키가 작고
그렇다고 찔레꽃인가 했더니
그보다는 더 크고 화사한 순백의 우아함이여
막 샘물에 세수하고 나온 듯
해말간 옥양목 치마저고리 곱게 차려 입은
울 엄마 같은
홀로 어둠 속에서도 그 빛이 우뚝하여 고광일까
진동하는 그의 향기에 취해 나는 그만 넋을 잃고 말았네

Wild Viburnum

As spring flowers bloom and fade,
bloom and fade again,
and the world ripples with fresh green,
I met you in a mountain valley.
From afar,
I thought you might be a magnolia,
but closer up, you were smaller,
and not quite a wild rose either —
you stood between the two,
graceful in your pure white elegance.
As if you had just washed your face
in a spring,
dressed neatly in a skirt and jacket
of fresh cotton —
you looked just like my mother.
Even alone in the dark,
your light stands tall.
Perhaps that is why
they call you Gogwang,
for your brightness.
Drunk on your fragrance,
I lost myself completely.

내 마음 속 꽃밭

봄이 오면
찔레꽃으로
여름이 오면
달리아로 피었다가
가을이 오면
쑥부쟁이로
겨울이 오면
동백꽃으로
당신은
아득히 먼 곳에
계시지만
아직도 당신은
내 마음 속 꽃밭에
사시사철
살아 계십니다

The Flower Garden in My Heart

When spring comes,

you bloom as wild roses.

When summer arrives,

you flower as dahlias.

When autumn comes,

you become asters.

When winter arrives,

you bloom as camellias.

Though you dwell

in a place far, far away,

you still live on,

in the flower garden of my heart,

through all four seasons.

낙화

해마다
지천으로 피고 지는 게 꽃이니
설령
저 눈부신 꽃들이
와르르 한꺼번에
무너져 내린다 한들
절대
서러워 말 일이다

우리네 인생 한 번 가면
그 찬란했던 봄날은
다시 돌아올 길 없으니
어찌 아니 서러우랴
두 번 다시 피울 수 없는 인생
후회 없이
즐기다 갈 일이로다

Falling Blossoms

Year after year

flowers bloom and scatter

in profusion — so even if

those dazzling blooms

were to collapse

all at once

there is no reason to grieve.

For in our lives,

once a season passes,

the radiant days of spring

can never return.

How could the heart not feel sorrow?

A life that will never

blossom twice —

let us savor it fully,

and depart without regret.

바람은 요술쟁이

보드라운 바람 불어와
윤슬이 반짝이던 서귀포 앞바다에
갑작스런 돌풍을 일으켜
가파도 바닷길을 끊어놓기도 하고
느닷없이 태풍을 몰고 와서
제주 하늘길을 끊어놓다가도
어김없이 남풍이 불어와 산방산 허리를 휘휘 감돌아
겨울잠에 취해 있던 마늘밭 새싹들을 일깨우고
유채밭에 들러서 벌 나비 떼 불러모아
한바탕 노랑 봄 잔치를 벌이는 바람은 요술장이

The Wind Is a Magician

A gentle wind blows,
and the shimmer on the sea
before Seogwipo sparkles —
then suddenly it whips up fierce gusts,
cutting off the sea route to Gapado.
At times, without warning,
it drives in a typhoon,
closing the skies over Jeju.
Yet unfailingly,
when the south wind returns,
it coils around the waist of Sanbangsan,
wakes the garlic shoots
drowsing in winter fields,
lingers in the canola rows,
summoning bees and butterflies
to stage a yellow estival of spring.

The wind is a true magician.

화살나무 1

쏜살같은 세월
사랑만 하고 살아도
부족한 세상
밉다고
죽도록 밉다고
아무에게나
화살을
겨눌 일이 아닙니다
함부로 쏜 화살이
부메랑이 되어
당신의 심장에
꽂힐 수도 있느니
미움을
오래 품지 말고
마음 속에
사랑을 키우면
행복의
꽃이 만발하리니
우리 모두
가슴 속에
사랑의 꽃씨를 품고
살아갈 일입니다

Spindle Tree I

Time flies like an arrow.
Even a lifetime spent only in love
would still be too short in this world.

Do not, in hatred —
hatred so fierce it feels fatal —
aim your arrows at just anyone.
An arrow loosed in recklessness
may return as a boomerang
and pierce your own heart.

Do not harbor resentment for long.
If you nurture love within your heart,
flowers of happiness will bloom in abundance.
So let us all live our lives
carrying seeds of love
deep within our chests.

나 홀로 나무

몽촌토성 언덕배기
나 홀로 나무
낮에는 멧새들이 놀러와서
외로움을 달래주고
밤에는 별들과 눈 맞춤하며
무서움을 견뎌내고
세찬 비바람이나
눈보라가 몰아닥쳐도
나 홀로 우뚝 서서
아리랑 아리랑 홀로 아리랑
오늘도 희망찬 내일을 향해
세상 풍파 거친 파도
헤쳐 나간다

The Lone Tree

On a hillside of Mongchon Fortress,
a lone tree.
By day, wild birds come to play,
easing its loneliness.
By night, it locks eyes
with the stars, enduring the fear.
Though fierce winds blow,
though snowstorms rage,
it stands tall, alone —
Arirang, Arirang, singing alone.
Even today,
toward a hopeful tomorrow,
it braves the rough waves
of this storm-tossed world.

화살나무 2

여름 내내
잎이 하도 무성하여
도무지
그 속내를 알 수 없더니
늦가을이 되어서야
마침내
그 속을 드러내기
시작하는구나
하늘을 향한 화살 촉들이
시위를 떠나는 순간
허공을 헤메이다가
자칫 그 화살이
당신에게로 돌아와
당신의 심장에
박히는 순간
온통
피투성이가 된
당신의 사랑은
미완성인 채
끝나버릴지도
모르는 일
시위를 함부로
당길 일이 아니로다

Spindle Tree 2

All summer long,
its leaves were so dense
that you could not know
what lay hidden within.
Only in late autumn
does it finally begin
to reveal its inner truth.

Arrowheads aimed at the sky —
the moment they leave the bowstring,
they drift through empty air,
and in a fatal instant
may turn back toward you,
burying themselves in your heart.

Then your love,
entirely soaked in blood,
may come to an end —
unfinished.

One must not
draw the bowstring lightly.

담장이 덩굴의 꿈

음습하고
쾌쾌한 냄새는 둘째 치고
한 조각 하늘과
한 뼘의 햇빛이
얼마나 소중하고
한 움큼의 바람이
얼마나 절절한지
그 심정
지하 셋방살이를
겪어본 사람은 누구나 안다
죽기 전에
하늘을 보고야 말겠다는
일념으로
옹벽을 기어오르다
떨어지면
다시 또 기어오르고
마침내
어두운 늪을 벗어나
하늘 한 조각을
가슴에 품는 순간
온 세상을 다 얻은 듯
세상 부러울 게 또 뭐가 있으랴
무슨 일이고 끝장을 볼 때까지
나의 사전엔 절대 포기란 없습니다

The Dream of a Wall Lizard

Leaving aside the damp
and the stale smell,
how precious a fragment of sky,
how dear a span of sunlight,
how aching a handful of wind —

anyone who has lived underground
knows this.
Before death,
with one fierce resolve
to see the sky,
I climb the wall.
I fall, and climb again.
At last,
out of the dark marsh,
holding one piece of sky
to my chest,
it feels as if I have gained
the whole world.
What then is left to envy?
Whatever the matter,
to the very end,
my dictionary contains no word
for surrender.

숨 쉴 권리

모든 생물에게는 다 저마다 누리고 살아갈
생존권이 있을 터인데 비록 몰지각한 인간들에게
무저항으로 짓밟혀도 잘 버티며 살아왔는데 머잖아
파릇파릇 새 생명이 태어날 저 잔디들의
숨 쉴 권리를 빼앗아버리면 도대체 어쩌란 말이냐
우수도 지났으니 경정장 얼음도 때가 되면
제풀에 풀릴텐데 일부러 쇄빙선까지 동원하여
그 깨부순 얼음 조각들을 잔디밭에 쏟아부어
저들의 숨통을 끊어버리다니
지각없는 인간들의 패악질은
도대체 언제 끝이 날까요

The Right to Breathe

Every living being has its own right to live.
Trampled without resistance by senseless humans,
they have endured.
But if you take away the right to breathe
from the lawns where fresh green lives
are about to be born — what then?
The ice would have melted in its own time.
Yet you shattered it on purpose,
spilled the broken cold onto the grass,
and cut off their breath.
When will human thoughtlessness ever end?

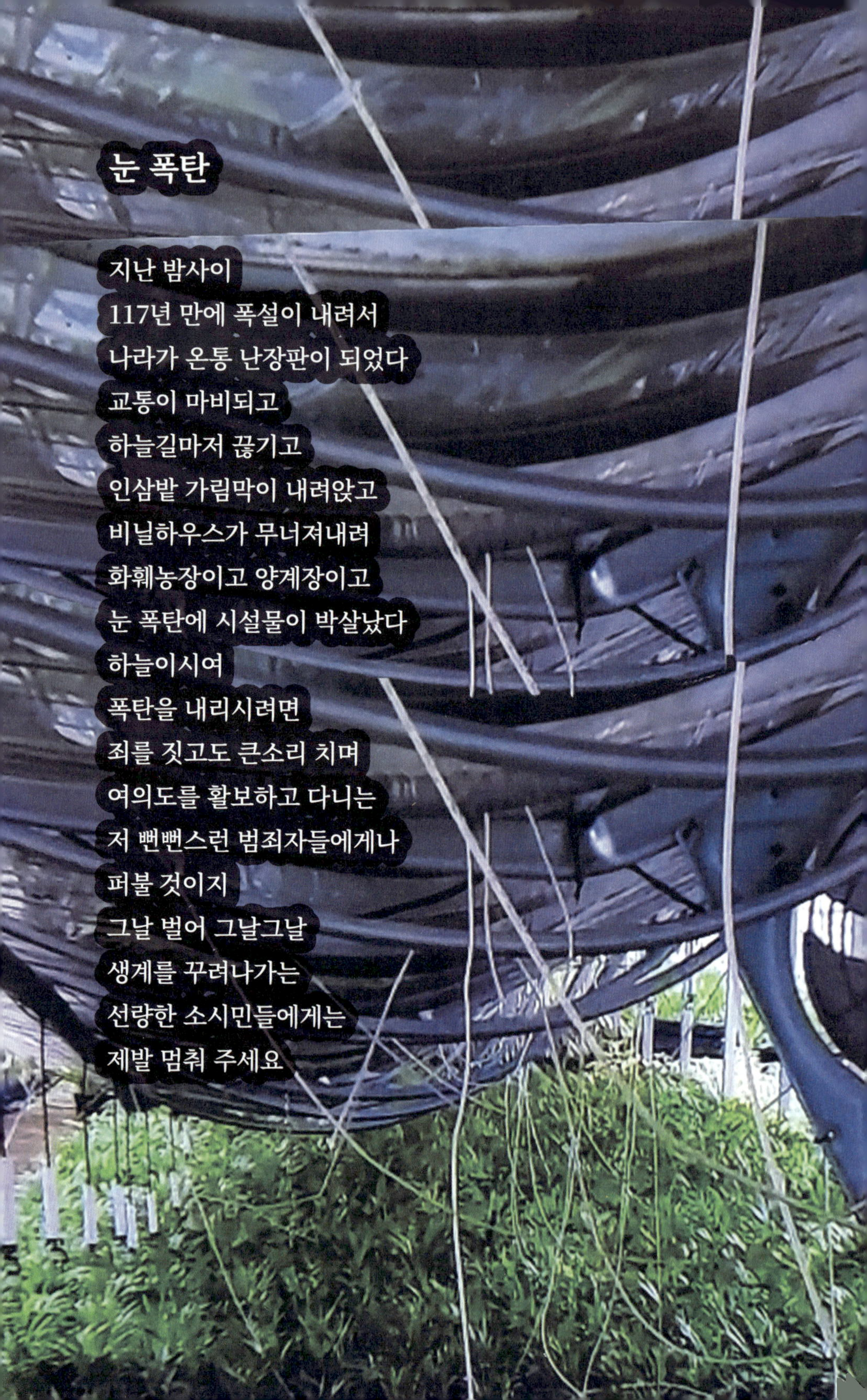

눈 폭탄

지난 밤사이
117년 만에 폭설이 내려서
나라가 온통 난장판이 되었다
교통이 마비되고
하늘길마저 끊기고
인삼밭 가림막이 내려앉고
비닐하우스가 무너져내려
화훼농장이고 양계장이고
눈 폭탄에 시설물이 박살났다
하늘이시여
폭탄을 내리시려면
죄를 짓고도 큰소리 치며
여의도를 활보하고 다니는
저 뻔뻔스런 범죄자들에게나
퍼불 것이지
그날 벌어 그날그날
생계를 꾸려나가는
선량한 소시민들에게는
제발 멈춰 주세요

Snow Bomb

Overnight, for the first time in 117 years,
a record blizzard fell,
throwing the entire country into chaos.
Traffic came to a standstill,
even the skies were sealed shut.
Ginseng field shelters collapsed,
plastic greenhouses caved in —
flower farms, poultry houses,
their facilities shattered by a snow bomb.

O Heaven,
if you must rain down your bombs,
pour them instead
on those shameless criminals
who commit their crimes
yet strut loudly through Yeouido.
For the innocent small citizens
who earn their living day by day,
for those who survive hand to mouth —
please,

산책길 풍경 1

휠체어를 타고 다녀야 할 할머니가
되레
유모차에 강아지를 태우고
망월천 산책길을
위태롭게 걸어가신다
두런두런
강아지와 이야기를 나누며
'아가야 저 하늘 좀 보아라
어느새 여름이 가고
가을이 왔구나'
'아가야
저 들꽃들 좀 보아라
앙증맞은 게 꼭
우리 아가만큼 예쁘구나'
할머니는 말벗이 되어주는
강아지가
멀리 사는 아들 손주보다
더 귀엽고 사랑스러울까만
등 뒤로
흘러내리는 외로움은
다 어찌 할거나

A Scene on the Walking Path 1

A grandmother
who ought to be riding a wheelchair
instead pushes a stroller,
a little dog inside,
and walks unsteadily
along the Mangwol Stream path.
She chatters softly with the dog.
"Little one, look at that sky —
summer has slipped away,
and autumn has arrived."
"Little one, look at those wildflowers —
so tiny and sweet,
almost as pretty
as my own baby."
Is the dog,
who keeps her company,
more precious and dear
than the son and grandchildren
who live far away?
Yet the loneliness
spilling down her bent back —
whatever shall be done with that?

웃어야 할까 울어야 할까

쌍둥이로 태어나서
누가 누가 잘 자라나
경쟁하며
하늘 높은 줄 모르고
쑥쑥 잘도 자랐지
사방팔방 팔을 뻗으며
푸르게 푸르게
우뚝 솟아올랐는데
독불장군
주변을 살피지 않고
하늘에
오르려는 욕심이
화근이 되었을까
우리 형제 그만
요모양 요꼴이
되었지만
지나는 사람들마다
멋지다고
감탄을 하며
발걸음을 멈추니
웃어야 할까
울어야 할까

Should We Laugh or Cry

Born a twin,
we grew up competing,
reaching higher and higher,
blind to the sky's limit.

We stretched our arms everywhere,
green and greener,
standing tall.

But our stubborn climb,
our hunger for the sky,
may have been our undoing.

Now my brother and I
are left like this —
yet strangers pause,
calling us magnificent.

So tell us,
should we laugh, or cry?

3부

관광여행 유감

강남 까치

드디어 인 서울
내남없이 부러워하는
강남에
집을 지었습니다
그것도
롯데월드 타워가
부럽지 않은
올림픽 대교 입구
최고의 일조권과
최고의 한강 뷰
게다가
최고의 종합병원과
잠실 역세권에
날마다
구름 위에서
해와 달과
별들을 거느리고
세상 부러울 것
하나 없는
나는야
강남 까치랍니다

Gangnam Magpie

Finally in Seoul

I built a house in *Gangnam,

the place everyone envies.

Not just any house,

but one that doesn't envy

the Lotte Tower,

right at the entrance

of the Olympic Bridge.

with the best sunlight,

the best view of the Han River,

and the best general hospital nearby,

right by Jamsil Station.

I live above the clouds,

with the sun, the moon, and stars

by my side, lacking nothing

the world might envy.

I am the Gangnam magpie.

*Gangnam : The South of the Han River

매미

최후 발악을 하는구나
숨마저 턱턱 막히는 말복 문턱에서
떠나는 여름이
뭐가 그리 아쉽다고
날 새기가 무섭게
애끓는 매미들의 절규가
새벽을 흔들어 깨운다
무슨 원한이 그리도 많은지
귀청을 찢을 듯
진종일 갈아대는 쇳소리가
저녁 어스름까지도 끊일 줄 모르고
푹푹 잇따라 삶아대는 열대야까지
오늘 밤도
단잠 자기는 영 글렀구나

Cicadas

You make your final desperate cries.
On the threshold
of the stifling heat of late summer,
as soon as day breaks,
the cicadas erupt in a chorus of wailing.
Drenched in sweat since dawn,
I wonder what grudges you carry,
your metallic screeches
grinding the air,
tearing at my eardrums,
never ceasing even into the twilight.
Through the sweltering tropical night,
tonight again,
a deep sleep is already lost.

엄지 척

좋아요
당신이 최고입니다
우리가 상대방을 칭찬할 때
흔히 엄지손가락을
번쩍 세우며 하는 말이지만
'칭찬은 고래도 춤을 추게 한다'고
이런 말을 듣는 사람이
용기 백배로
힘이 불끈 솟는다면
칭찬은 아무리 해도
절대로
아낄 일이 아니지만
듣기 좋은 칭찬도
지나치면
역효과를
가져올 수 있으니
적당한 칭찬이야말로
활기찬 삶의 원동력이
분명하니
엄지 척
서로 칭찬하는
하루가 됩시다

Thumbs Up

"Good," "You're the best!
These are words
we use to compliment others,
often raising a thumb —
sometimes both thumbs high.
But as they say,
"Praise makes even whales dance,"
those who hear such words
truly feel good, their courage boosted,
their strength renewed.
If praise can lead to growth and progress,
it's certainly not something to be held back.
Yet, for those who take pride in their views
on social media, or for most YouTubers
who, driven by self-interest,
are desperate to boost their views,
there's no denying the irony.
we all love hearing sweet words,
too much praise can have the opposite effect.
Isn't it the right balance of praise
that truly becomes the driving force of our lives?

열대야

장맛비가 끝나기가 무섭게
찾아온 찜통더위에
궁싯궁싯
귀잠 들지 못하고
밤새 뒤척이다가
새벽녘에야
겨우 그루잠이 든 사이
내 몸뚱이가
화장터 불구덩이 속으로 던져지는 꿈에
소스라쳐 깨어보니
온 몸이 땀으로 흥건하다
뭐니 뭐니 해도
잠이 보약이라고 했거늘
밤낮없이
냉풍기를 틀고 지낼 수도 없고
이 노릇을 어찌하면 좋으랴

Tropical Night

No sooner had the monsoon rains passed
than the sweltering heat came rushing in.
I toss and turn all night,
too restless to drift into a proper sleep,
dozing off at last near dawn —
only to dream my body
was flung into the roaring flames
of a crematory.
I wake in a jolt,
drenched in sweat from head to toe.
They say
nothing heals like a good night's rest,
but how can I endure
when I can't keep the cool air running
day and night?
What on earth am I to do?

빈 배

오랜 세월
길손들의
수많은 사연을 싣고
강을 거슬러
오르내리던 나룻배가
주인을 잃어버린 채
마구 세월에 떠밀려서
미동도 없이 그만
시간 속에 갇혀버렸다
바람도
구름도 숨 죽이고
세상 모든 게 다
멈춰버렸지만
재깍재깍
시계바늘은
쉼 없이 돌아가고
지구도 돌고 돌아
역사는 흘러만 가고
나도 속절없이
세월에 떠밀려
늙어만 가는구려

Empty Boat

For countless years
ferrying the endless stories
of passing travelers,
the river boat that once
climbed and drifted
along the current
has now lost its master.
Driven aimlessly by time,
it lies motionless,
trapped inside the hours.

The wind holds its breath,
the clouds stand still,
as though the whole world
has stopped —
yet the clock's hands
tick on without rest,
the earth keeps circling,
history keeps flowing,
and I, too, helplessly
am carried along by time,
growing old.

불면증

이리 뒤척 저리 뒤척
밤새 궁싯거리다가
새벽으로 갈수록
두 눈은 점점 더 말똥 말똥
아무리 잠을 청해봐도
잠은 이미
십리 밖으로
달아나버리고
끝내 건 밤으로
밤을 하얗게
밝히고 나니
온통 세상이 다
어질어질
고문이
따로 없네
그러게
늙어가면서
보약이
뭐 별거더냐
잠만 잘 자면
그 게 바로
보약인 것을

Insomnia

I toss and turn,
this way, that way,
fussing all night long.
As dawn draws nearer,
my eyes only grow wider —
bright as a startled calf's.

No matter how I beg for sleep,
it has already fled ten miles away.
In the end, I keep vigil through the night,
bleaching the darkness white.

When morning comes,
the whole world spins —
a torture, nothing less.

So yes, as we grow old,
what is a tonic, really?
Nothing special at all:
to sleep well —
that alone is the true medicine.

미소 1

내 사진을 정리하다 보니
모두 벌레 씹은 얼굴 아니면
꺼벙한 모습이 꼭 뭔가 못 마땅한 표정들 뿐이다
사진을 찍을 때마다
아내는 내게 웃으라고
김치며 치즈를 외쳐대지만
찍고 보면 늘 그 표정이 그 표정인 것을
이제 와서 어찌할거나

Smile 1

While organizing old photos,

I realized —

not a single good one.

If it's not a bug-chewed face,

it's a dopey expression,

or a look that seems somehow

dissatisfied.

At every famous spot

during our travels,

my wife would urge me to smile,

shouting

"Kimchi" or "Cheese !"

but every shot

turned out the same.

Joy or sorrow,

I've never been one

to wear my heart on my face —

and now.

What can I do abut it?

미소 2

나와는 달리
내 아내는 늘 잘 웃는다
내가 듣기에는
하나도 우습지 않은 이야기도
말도 꺼내기 전에 배꼽부터 잡고 웃느라고
말도 제대로 못 할 만큼 웃음이 많은 여자이다
어쩌면 내가 이 나이 먹도록
행복을 누리고 사는 것도 다 아내 덕이 아닐까 싶어
새삼 아내에게 고맙다는 생각을 떨칠 수 없다

Smile 2

Unlike me,
my wife always laughs easily.
Even at stories that sound to me
not funny at all,
she clutches her belly in laughter
before the words are even out,
laughing so hard
she can barely finish a sentence.

Perhaps the happiness I have enjoyed,
even at this age,
is all thanks to her.
The thought keeps returning —
how grateful I am to my wife.

경로석

전철을 타면
경로석 빈자리를 외면하고
출입문 언저리에서
어중간하게 서서 다니던 내가
언제부터인가

경로석을 엿보기 시작하더니
이제는
누가 자리를 내어주지 않을까
두리번거리는 지경에 이르렀다
'누죽걸산'이라고
집에만 쳐박혀 지낼 수도 없고
그렇다고
차를 몰고 나갈 수도 없고
나는 '지공선사' 오늘도 룰루랄라
전철역을 향하여 발걸음을 재촉한다

* 누죽걸산: 누(우면) 죽(고) 걸(으면) 산(다)
* 지공선사: 지하철을 공짜로 타는 만65세 이상의 노인

Priority Seat

When I used to ride the subway,
even if
there was a vacant priority seat,
I wouldn't sit.
I would stand awkwardly near the door.
But at some point,
when I take the subway now,
I start glancing at the priority seats,
and lately, I even find myself
looking around — wondering
if someone might offer me a seat.
"They say if you lie down, you die —
if you walk, you live.
"I can't just stay cooped up at home,
but I can't drive around either.
I've become a *Jigong Seonsa,
with no choice but to ride.
Today again, I go "lululala,"
heading to the subway station

* Jigong Seonsa : The Free Subway Zen Master

행방이 묘연한 모자

내둥 잘도 쓰고 다니던 모자가
어느 날 그 행방이 묘연해졌다
금방 들은 소리도 돌아서면 잊어버리는
그런 나이가 되긴 했어도
들고 다니던 우산이며 장갑 한 짝도
잃어버린 적이 없던 내가
이제 죽을 때가 다 되었나보라고
구시렁거리는 나에게
내다버려도 아무도 주워가지 않을
그까짓 것 가지고
몇 날을 구시렁거리고 다닌다고
마누라는 나에게 핀잔하지만
그까짓 것 남 보기엔 하찮아 보여도
나에겐 얼마나 소중한 물건인데
두고두고 아쉬운 마음이 가시지 않는다

The Hat That Went Missing

The hat I used to wear so well
one day vanished without a trace.
Though I've reached the age
when a sound just heard
is forgotten the moment I turn away,
I was never one
to lose an umbrella I carried
or even a single glove.
So perhaps
I'm nearing the end of my days —
that's what I grumble to myself.
My wife scolds me, saying
no one would bother picking up
something like that
even if it were thrown away,
and that fretting over it
for days on end
is hardly worth the trouble.
But that something,
though it may look trivial to others,
was precious to me.
The feeling of loss
lingers, and will not easily fade.

관광여행 유감

나의 어머니는 열아홉에
대가족 맏며느리로 시집와서
삭정이로 불 지펴 가마솥에 밥 짓고
손빨래하고 나면 들에 나가 밭농사까지
우리 육 남매 기르시느라
관광여행은 언감생심
하루도 허리 펼 날
없으셨다는데
요즈음 주부들은
밥은 전기밥솥이
빨래는 세탁기가
집안 청소는
로봇이 게다가
들 일은커녕
남편 출근하면
눈치 볼 사람
하나 없이
늘어진 팔자인데도
여행만 나오면
이구동성
밥상 안 차려서
세상 좋다고 하니
참 세상 변해도
많이 변했구나

The Regret of Sightseeing

My mother, at just nineteen,

married into a big family

as the eldest daughter-in-law.

She lit fires with dry twigs,

cooked rice in a cauldron,

scrubbed clothes by hand —

then headed to the fields to farm.

Raising six of us,

a sightseeing trip was

beyond her wildest dreams.

Not a single day, they say, did her back know

the feeling of straightening.

But housewives these days —

the rice is cooked by electric pots,

the laundry done by machines.

They don't step foot in the fields,

and once the husband's off to work,

no one left to mind or please.

A leisurely life, yet every time they travel,

they all say in unison:

"How wonderful not having to set the table!"

Truly, how the world has changed so much.

하소연

등대 : 친구들은 다 어데 가고 너 혼자 외롭지 않니?
갈매기 : 외롭지 않다면 거짓말이지. 너는 안 외롭니?
등대 : 사실 나는 중병에 걸려서 외로울 시간도 없어
갈매기 : 무슨 병인데?
등대 : 연예인 병. 사람들이 늦은 밤까지 찾아와서
같이 사진 찍자고 귀찮게 구는 통에
편히 잠 잘 시간도 없어
갈매기 : 그렇구나.
내 친구들은 새우깡에
길들여져서
늘 관광객들의
눈치만 살피느라고
나는 것도 포기 하고
죄다 무기력해졌어
등대 : 그러게 몰지각한
인간들 때문에 바다가
병 들어가는 것도
안타깝고
오나가나 인간들이
문제로구나

A Lament

Lighthouse: Where have all your friends gone?
   Aren't you lonely here, all by yourself?
Seagull : I'd be lying if I said I wasn't.
   Aren't you lonely?
Lighthouse : Truth is, I'm seriously ill —
   I don't even have time to feel lonely.
Seagull : What kind of illness?
Lighthouse : Celebrity disease.
   People come until late at night,
   pestering me to take photos together.
   I don't even get a proper night's sleep.
Seagull : I see.
   My friends have grown addicted
   to shrimp crackers,
   forever watching tourists' moods.
   They've even given up flying —
   all of them sunk into lethargy.
Lighthouse : Exactly.
   It's heartbreaking
   to see the sea itself falling ill
   because of thoughtless humans.
   Wherever you go, whenever you look —
   in the end, it's humans who are the problem.

개만도 못한 인간들

사룟값이 없다고 애완견을 버리는 사람이 있는가 하면
그 유기견을 데려와 한 식구처럼 사는 사람도 있다
사람은 개를 배반하더라도 개는 주인집을 밤낮 지켜주며
위험에 처한 주인을 구했다는 인터넷 소식을 접할 때마다
개만도 못한 사람들 보다 훌륭한 개가 더 많은 세상이라니
눈만 뜨면 거짓말을 밥 먹듯 하는
양심 없는 인간들이여
제발 대한민국을 떠나거라
아니 아예 이 지구를 떠나거라

Humans Worse Than Dogs

Some cast away their dogs
claiming the cost of feed is too much.
Others gather those castaways
and call them family.

A human may betray a dog,
but a dog never abandons a home —
keeping watch through day and night,
even risking its life to save its master,
so the stories tell us.

Each time I read them,
I realize this is a world
where noble dogs outnumber
humans who have sunk beneath them.

You who greet each morning
with lies already on your tongue,
you who live without shame —
leave this land called Korea.

No,
leave this Earth itself.

강남을 지나며

돈을 얹어주면 모를까
거저 준다 해도
누구 하나 거들떠보지도 않던
아무짝에도 쓸모없던
뽕밭이나 모래밭이
저렇게 하늘을 찌르는 빌딩 숲이 될줄이야
애먼 서울 땅을
남과 북으로 갈라놓은 한강이
저주스럽다는 나의 푸념에
등 따숩고 배부르고 게다가
자식들 무탈하게 잘 자랐으면
행복한 줄 알아야지
뭔 놈의 욕심이 그리도 하늘을 찌르느냐며
생전 사촌이 땅을 사도
배 아픈 줄을 모르던 마누라가
나에게 뼈 아픈 오금을 박는다
"도대체 저 사람은 배알도 없는 걸까
아니면 부활하신 예수라도 되는 걸까?"
갑자기
마누라가 하늘처럼 우러러 보였다

Passing Through Gangnam

Unless you added money on top,
no one would glance twice —
those useless fields of mulberry or sand,
Who could have imagined
they would become
this forests of buildings piercing the sky.
The Han River,
which blindly split Seoul
into North and South,
was the target of my bitter complaints.
But my wife, warm, full-bellied,
her children growing well —
said I should count my blessings.
Why let your greed reach for the sky?
She shoots me a piercing jab:
"Is that woman completely shameless?
Or is she the resurrected
Jesus herself?"
Suddenly, I looked up to my wife
as if she were the sky itself.

물거품

바다가
시뻘건 불덩이를 삼키고
밤새 속앓이를 하더니
식전 댓바람부터
성난 파도가 토해낸
물거품들이
떠돌다 떠돌다가 그만
아침 햇살에
흔적도 없이
사그라들고야 만다
우리네 인생도
때로는
거친 세파에 시달리며
떠돌다 떠돌다가 그만
사그라드는
물거품이런가
미련도
후회도 없이
사라져버리고 마는
신기루
허무하고 허무한
인생은 신기루이런가

Foam

The sea swallows the blood-red sun,

wrestles with its heartburn

through the night,

and at the break of dawn,

spits up frothing waves in fury.

bubbles drift, wander

under the morning light,

they vanish without a trace.

Is this what life is?

Tossed by rough tides,

adrift and adrift again —

only to dissolve, just like foam?

No regret,

no longing,

no trace left behind —

a mirage, flickering and gone.

Ah, this hollow, hollow life.

역마살

이사를 하도 잘 다니는 우리를
부동산 투기의 귀재라고
놀려대는 사람도 있지만
어쩌랴
역마살이라도 끼었을까
우리 부부
한 곳에 오래 머물지 못 하고
이리저리 떠돌아다니는 방랑벽은
닮아도 너무 닮아서
이번이 마지막이라고
다짐하며
용인에서 하남으로
떠나갔었지만
그사이에 남양주로
거기에서
또다시 용인으로
이러다가 우리 부부
길바닥에서
죽을지도 모르지만
이 또한 어쩌랴
아무데나
정 붙이고 누우면
거기가 다
내 집인 것을

Wanderer's Fate

Some people sneer
that we are geniuses
of real-estate speculation,
since we move so often.
But what can we do —
perhaps we are marked
with a wanderer's fate.
My spouse and I,
unable to stay long in one place,
roaming here and there —
our restlessness so alike
it is almost uncanny.
Each time we vow,
this will be the last,
and leave Yongin for Hanam,
only to drift on to Namyangju,
and then once again back to Yongin.
At this rate,
we may end up dying on the roadside —
but again, what can we do?
Wherever we grow attached,
wherever we lie down,
that place becomes our home.

Walking to Heaven

4부

걸어서
하늘까지

감사

이 나이 먹도록
두 다리로 대지를 딛고
내 마음껏
쏘다닐 수 있어서 감사
이 나이 먹도록
두 눈으로
우주 삼라만상을
내 마음껏
눈 호강 할 수 있어서
또 감사
이 나이 먹도록
건강한 치아로 맛난 거
내 마음껏
호식할 수 있어서
또 또 감사
그 무엇보다
매일 아침 눈을 떠서
하루하루
무탈하게 지내고
저녁
잠자리에 들 수 있어서
그저 무한 감사

Gratitude

Grateful —
that at this age,
I still stand on two legs,
roaming the earth freely.
Grateful —
that at this age, with two eyes,
I can feast upon the wonders
of the boundless universe.
Grateful —
that at this age, with strong teeth,
I can savor every bite
of delicious things.
And above all —
grateful simply
to open my eyes each morning,
to pass the day in peace,
and to rest at night, safe and sound.
Just deeply, tremendously grateful.

누죽걸산 2

세월 이길 장사 없다고
하루가 다르게
몸이 매시근하고
정신마저 우련하며
머릿속이 하얘져서
어제 일조차
까마득하다
첫눈이 내리려나
날씨마저 꾸무럭대니
도무지
바깥에 나가기가
저어하지만
그럴 때마다
'누죽걸산'
용맹히
자리를 박차고
집을 나선다
처자식 걱정
덜어주기 위해서라도
무념무상
그저 걷고 또 걷고

Lie Down and You Die, Walk and You Live 2

"They say no one can beat time."

Day by day,my body grows weary,

and even my mind feels dim.

My head goes blank —

even yesterday is a blur.

Perhaps the first snow will fall soon.

With the sky brooding gray,

stepping outside

feels like such a chore.

But suddenly,

"Lie down and you die,

walk and you live"

comes to mind.

I leap from my seat,

hurry out the door,

and walk, walk again —

if only to ease

my family's worry.

이 세상 끝날에

내둥 잘 다니던 길에서
갑자기
돌부리에 차여 넘어졌지만
다행히 팔다리가 멀쩡하다
안도의 한숨을 내쉬면서
나도 모르게
튀어나온 말
'하느님 감사 합니다'

하루하루
무탈함이
다 감사할 일인데
하늘 한 번
쳐다보지 않고
거만 떨고 다니다가
위험에
맞닥뜨릴 때마다
하느님을 찾는
나같은 인간도
구원을
받을 수 있을까요
이 세상 끝날에

At the End of This World

I was walking along a path

I had trodden so well,

when suddenly, I tripped

over a hidden stone.

But — thankfully —

my arms and legs were unhurt.

With a sigh of relief,

I blurted out without thinking,

"Thank you, Lord."

Every single day

without mishap is a blessing

to be grateful for,

Yet I go about, head held high,

never once looking up

to the sky —

until danger finds me,

and I cry out to God.

Could even someone like me

be saved

at the end of this world?

기도

늙어가면서
병으로 고생 끝에
요양병원 신세 지느니
차라리
죽는 게 낫다는 말은
말짱 거짓말
환자들로 북새통인 종합병원에
가 본 적이 있는가
죽음의 그림자가
짙게 드리운 환자들
수액 줄을 주렁주렁 매달고
검사실 앞에서 차례를 기다리며
오로지
기적이 일어나기만 바라는 절박함에
저마다
마음속 깊이
두 손을 모은다
단 하루라도 더 살고 싶은
간절한 소망 하나로

Prayer

As they grow old,
the elderly often say
they'd rather die
than suffer long from illness
and end up in a nursing home —
but those words are utter nonsense.
Have you ever been to a general hospital,
crowded with patients?
There, under the heavy shadow of death,
the sick dangle IV lines
like withered branches,
waiting their turn
outside the examination room,
each of them, desperately hoping
for nothing but a miracle,
pressing their hands together
in the depths of their hearts —
all for the single, earnest wish
to live just one more day.

맨발 걷기 1

내가 수행자의 도를 닦는
비장한 결심으로
신발을 벗어 던지고
황톳길에 첫발을 내딛는 순간
심장에 칼끝이 찔린 듯
악 소리가 튀어나왔지만
맨발로
천연덕스럽게 걷거나
심지어
날다람쥐처럼
뛰어다니는 사람들을
보면서
발동한 오기
죽기 아니면
까무러치기라
이제는 비명 대신
그나마
두 발로 걸을 수 있음에
감사하며
오늘도
금대산 황톳길을 걷는다
신발을 벗어 던진 채

Barefoot Walking 1

With the heart of a monk in training,
I flung off my shoes
and took my first step
onto the cold clay path.
It felt like a blade piercing my heart —
a cry escaped, sharp and sudden.
But watching others walk with ease,
some even leaping like flying squirrel,
my pride kicked in.
Gritting my teeth,
I pressed on
as if my life depended on it.
Now, instead of screams,
I walk with gratitude —
thankful just to move
on my own two feet.
Today again, I hum a cheerful tune
and walk the clay road of Mt. Geumdae
with my shoes cast aside.

맨발 걷기 2

가슴 속까지 파고드는 동짓달 칼바람을
방풍 옷으로 감싸고
바닷물에 첫발을
내딛는 순간
머릿속까지
뻐근하게
아려오는 통증

내 몸에 찾아든
불청객을
내쫓으려면
이 정도
고통쯤이야

오늘도
죽자사자
이를 악물고
바닷길을 걷는다
무릎까지
바지를
걷어부친 채

Barefoot Walking 2

Wrapping the biting midwinter wind
that pierces my chest
in windproof clothes,
I take my first step into the sea —
a pain shoots through
to the back of my skull.

To drive out the unwelcome guest
that has crept into my body,
this kind of pains nothing.
So again today, gritting my teeth
as if life depends on it,
I walk the seashore,
pants rolled upto my knees.

미사

일요일 성당에 나가기 전에
먼저
단정한 몸가짐으로
자기 반성과
성찰은커녕
스마트폰만 만지작거리며
어영부영하다가 그만
미사 시간에 쫓겨서
부랴부랴
입던 옷을 그대로 걸치고
마누라 손에 끌려나간 성당
신부님 강론은 소귀에 경 읽기이고
우거지상으로 앉아서
이제나저제나
미사가 빨리 끝나기만 간절할 뿐이라
니체아 신경은커녕 주님의 기도도
더듬적거리는 40년 차 나와 같은 신앙 지진아도
세상 끝날에 구원 받을 수 있을까요

Mass

Before heading to church on Sunday,
instead of tidying myself
or offering a moment of self-reflection,
I just fumble with my smartphone,
dawdling about —
then end up rushed by the Mass hour,
throwing on whatever I was wearing
and being dragged out the door
by my wife's hand.

The priest's homily
goes in one ear and out the other.
I sit there with a sullen face,
desperately wishing
the Mass would end already.

I stumble even over the Lord's Prayer,
let alone the Nicene Creed —
a faith cripple like me,
forty years in belief:
when the end of the world comes,
will someone like me
still be saved?

끝날까지

함께 손잡고 걸어온
반백 년 세월
그 끝이 가까이 옴을
내 어찌 모르랴 만은
인정사정없이
이 세상 복이란 복
다 누리고 살았으니
당장
이 지구를 떠난다고 한들
여한이 없습니다
사랑하는 사람아
나 떠나거든
딱 삼 일만 눈물 쏟고
더이상 슬퍼 말고
굳굳하게 잘 지내다가
우리 천국에서 다시 만납시다
그때에는 내가
당신 손 꼭 잡고
당신을 여왕처럼 떠받들고 살리라

Until the Very End

Hand in hand we have walked
half a century together.
How could I not know
that the end is drawing near?

Yet I have lived, without mercy spared,
enjoying every blessing this world could give.
Even if I were to leave this earth today,
I would have no regrets.

My beloved,
when I am gone,
shed your tears for just three days—no more.
After that, grieve no longer.
Stand firm, live well,
until we meet again in heaven.

And then,
I will clasp your hand tightly
and live,
lifting you up
as my queen.

눈물의 십자가

하 추자도 신대산
갓바위 가는 길이
어찌나 험하던지
해안 둘레길을 따라
가시덤불을 헤치며
바윗고개를 넘고 넘어
죽을힘을 다하여
올라간 언덕 너머
거기서 또 당신은
너무도 아득하여
더이상
당신께로 다가가지 못하고
꿀꺽 꿀꺽
눈물만 삼키며
그냥 돌아서는 저를
불쌍히 여기시고
저의 죄를 죄다
용서해주시기만
빌 뿐입니다

The Cross of Tears

Hachuja-do —
the path to Gatbawi on Mount Sindae
was so terribly steep.
Following the coastal trail,
pushing through thorny thickets,
climbing over rocky passes,
crossing one ridge after another,
I pressed on with all the strength I had
until I reached the hill at last.

Beyond that rise,
You were still too distant,
so utterly beyond reach
that I could not step any closer to You.
Swallowing my tears,
again and again,
I could only turn back.

Have mercy on me,
pity this wretched soul,
and I beg You —
forgive all my sins.

그만하기 다행이다

내둥
잘 걸어 다니던 내가
그만 삐끗 발을 접질리어
발가락이 하나
골절되었다
반 깁스를 하고
며칠을
절뚝거리고 다니다가
급기야 철심을 박던 날
하느님께 제발
살려달라고
떼를 썼더니
"빨빨거리고 다니다가
그럴줄 알았다"고
나를 꾸짖으실 줄
알았는데
"그만하기 다행이다
팔십이 넘은 나이에
자칫
고관절이라도
부러졌으면
어쩔 뻔했느냐"고
되려
나를 위로해 주시다니
그저 하느님께
감사 드릴 따름이다

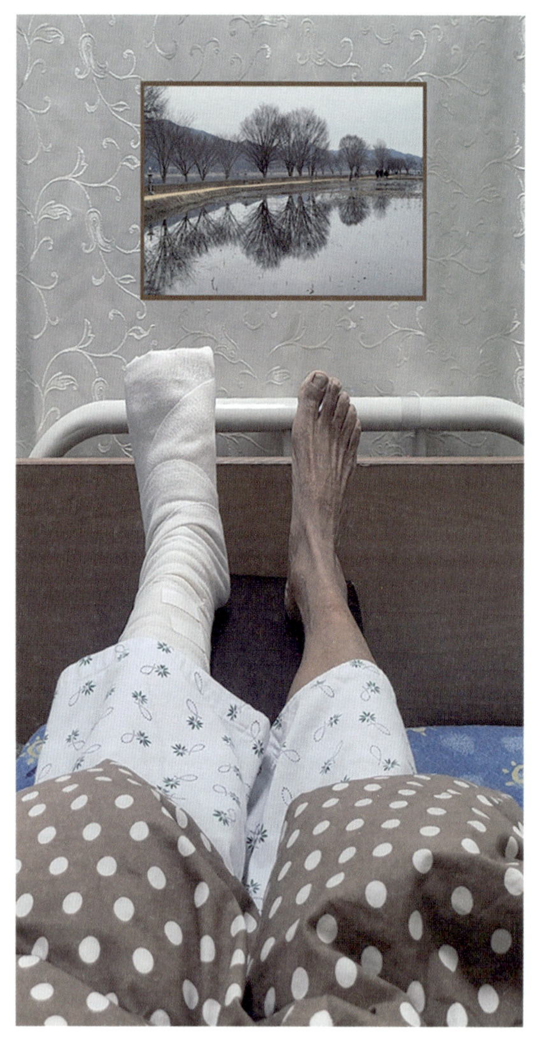

Lucky It Stopped There

One careless step —

though I had been walking just fine,

I twisted my foot

and broke a toe.

With a half-cast on,

I hobbled around for days,

until the day came

they put in a metal pin.

I begged the Lord,

"Please, spare me!"

Expecting Him to scold me —

"I knew you'd get in trouble,

always rushing about."

But instead He said,

"Be glad it stopped there.

At over eighty,

what if you had broken a hip?

What then?"

So I can only give thanks,

for such mercy.

동병상련

맨발의 청춘
저들은 신 노마드족이런가
가축은 거느리지 않았어도
구리선을 칭칭 감은
나무 지팡이를 양손에 짚고
황톳길을
오르락내리락
걷다가 힘이 들면
나뭇등걸에 걸터앉아
저마다
투병 노하우를 나누며
오늘도
동병상련의 하루가
또 저물어 간다

* 노마드 : 유목민

Kindred Struggles

Are those barefoot ones

some new kind of *nomads?

Though they herd no livestock,

they clutch staffs

coiled with copper wire

in both hands,

treading up and down

the clay-brown paths.

When weariness strikes,

they perchon a tree stump,

sharingbattle-worn wisdom,

as yet another day

of kindred struggle

fades into dusk.

*nomads : wanderers

하늘이시여

바닷물 속에 비친
낯선 얼굴 하나
여름내 시커멓게 그을리고
움푹 움푹 파인 주름살
검은 머리카락 휘날리며
산과 들을 내달리던 그 푸르던 날은
다 어데 가고
눈 내리는 겨울 바닷가를 서성이고 있을까
두 눈에 깊게 드리운 외로움은
그 누가 달래줄거나
하늘이시여
저 사람 가엽게 여기시어
그의 고통 어루만져 주시고
내일은
새 날 새 삶을 내려주소서

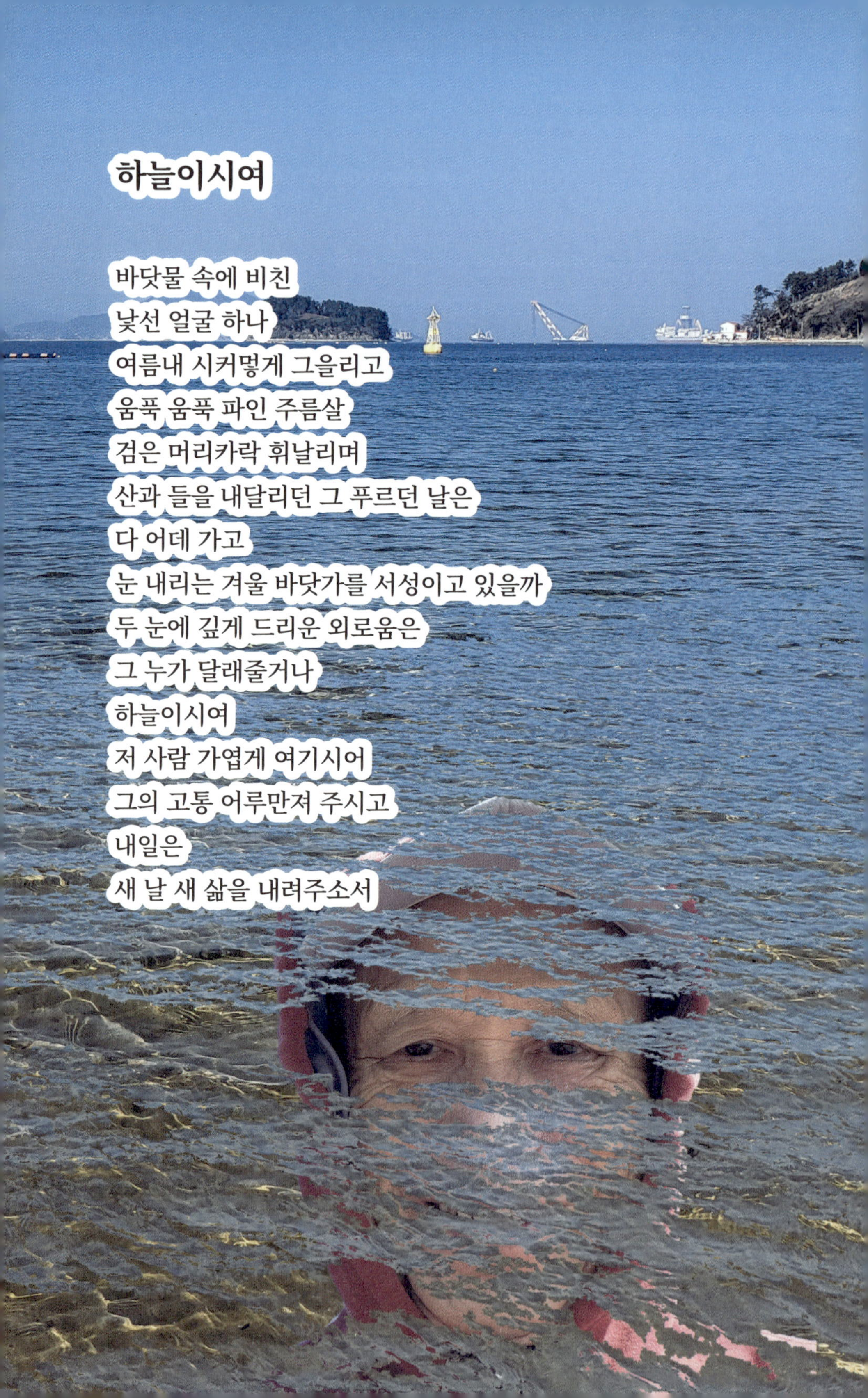

O Heaven

A stranger's face reflected in water —

all summer long,

burned bronze by the sun,

with furrows sunken deep.

Once, with dark hair streaming,

he ran through mountains and fields.

Where have those green

and gleaming days gone?

Does he now wander

the snow-swept shore

of a winter sea?

Who will calm

the loneliness shadowed

deep in his eyes?

O Heaven,

have pity on him,

lay your hand upon his sorrow —

and grant, I pray,

that tomorrow may be

a new day, a new life.

불청객

담당 의사로부터
방광암 통지를 받고 돌아오던 날
나에게도 피할 수 없이
찾아올 것이 왔구나
제멋대로 쏘다니며
건강을 뻐기고 으스댔던
지난 날의 자만심을
뼈저리게 반성하며
그나마
다른 암 환자들에
비하면
나는 유도 아니라고
외려
주변 사람들을
위로하며
애써 무덤덤한 체 해도
웬지 코끝이 찡하고
두 눈이 흐려져 옴은
몸이 지쳤기 때문만은
아닐 터
먼저 마음부터
단단히 먹고
불청객을 쳐부술
잡도리나 해야겠다

An Uninvited Guest

The day I came back after hearing
from the attending doctor
that it was bladder cancer,
I thought —
so it has come to me as well,
the thing no one can evade.
Wandering about as I pleased,
boasting of my health,
swaggering through my days,
I now bitterly repent
that old arrogance.
Compared with other cancer patients,
I tell myself I am fortunate,
even comforting those around me,
putting on a face of studied calm.
Yet for some reason
the tip of my nose stings,
my vision blurs —
surely not only because my body is tired.
First, I must steel my heart.
Then it is time to get a firm grip
and beat back
this uninvited guest.

입원

이 나이 되도록
남의 손가락질 안 당하고
잘 살아왔다 싶은데
갑자기
방광 속에 돋아난
암 덩어리 제거를 위해
입원을 하게 되었다
주삿바늘만 보아도
기겁하는 사람이
전신마취란
잠시 나를 죽인다는 것인데
다시 깨어날 수 있을지
두렵지 않을 수가 없지만
이 또한
당신의 뜻이라 여기고
온전히 나를
아버지의 손에 맡깁니다
주여
저의 모든 죄를
사하여 주소서

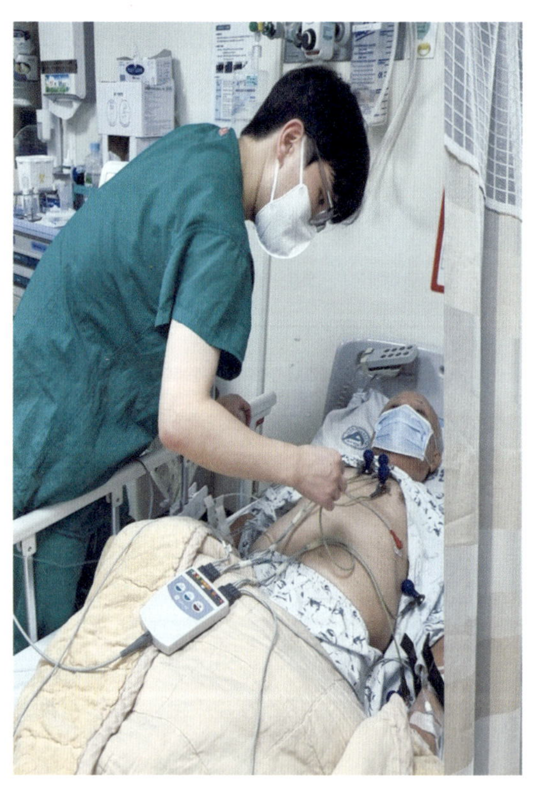

Hospitalization

All these years,

I thought I had lived well,

never giving anyone cause

to point a finger at me.

But suddenly,

to remove a lump of cancer

that sprouted in my bladder,

I have been admitted

to the hospital.

Even the sight of a needle

makes me shudder,

yet now they speak

of general anesthesia —

which means, for a while, to let myself die.

How could I not fear

that I might never awaken?

Still, I take this too as Your will,

and place myself wholly in the Father's hands.

Lord,

forgive me all my sins.

퇴원

아침식사 후 퇴원할 예정이다
아무리 무쇠로 만든 기계인들
80여년을 밤낮없이 돌아가다 보면
여기저기 고장이 나거나
멈춰섰을 터인데
하물며 관상동맥이 게다가
90퍼센트나
막힌 핏줄로
멈춰서지 않고
예까지 이르른 것만도
천운이었다는 생각 뿐
살려달라는
기도도 못했는데
나를 살려주시다니
하느님과
옆에서 기도와
걱정을 많이 한
엄마와
우리 삼남매 그리고
며느리 사위들에게
무한 감사할 따름이다

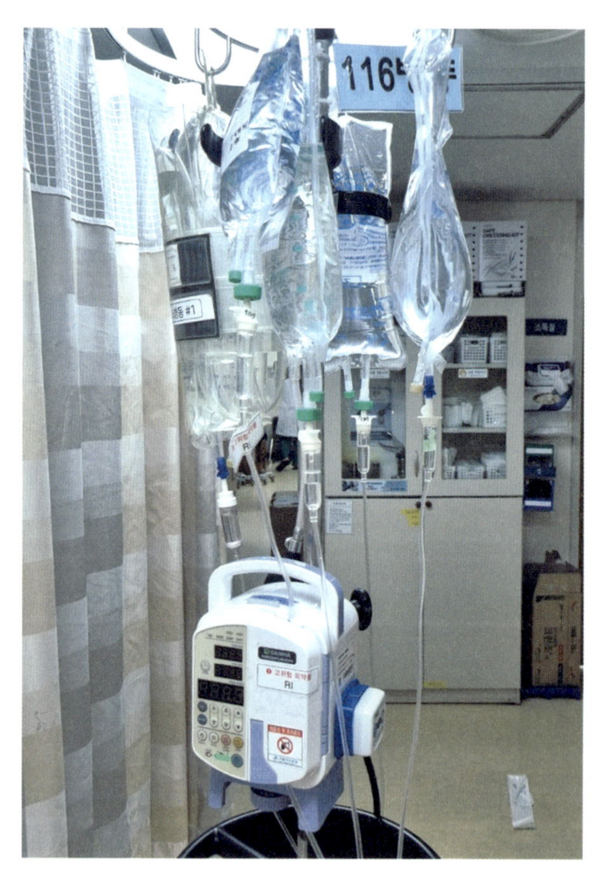

Discharge

After breakfast, I am to be discharged.
Even machines forged of iron,
after eighty years of ceaseless turning day and night,
would have broken down here and there,
or ground to a halt.

So how could I —
with coronary arteries narrowed by ninety percent —
have not stopped,
but come this far?
that alone feels like sheer, heaven-sent luck.

I never even managed a prayer asking to be spared,
yet I was spared.
To God,
and to your mother who prayed and worried beside me,
to my three siblings,
and to my daughter-in-law and son-in-law —
I offer only boundless gratitude.

걸어서 하늘까지

내 맘대로 쏘다니다가
설령
길바닥에서
쓰러진다 하여도
벗님네여
날 너무
불쌍히 여기지 마소
죽을까 겁이 나서
배도, 비행기도 못 타고
방구석에만 처박힌 채
오래 살아봐야
그 게
무슨 삶이란 말인가
다리 힘 빠져서
걷지도 못하고
요양원 신세나 지느니
지금 이대로 걷다가
그만 길 위에서
하늘나라로 직행한다면
보다 더 큰 축복이
어데 있으랴

Walking to Heaven

Even if I wander

wherever my feet may take me

and collapse one day

on the side of the road —

dear friends,

please don't pity me too much.

What kind of life is it,

to live long

yet be too afraid to die?

Too scared

to board a ship or plane,

just hiding away in the room?

Rather than wasting away

in a nursing home,

legs too weak to walk —

wouldn't it be

a far greater blessing

to keep walking,

just like this,

and head straight to heaven

from the open road?

해설

〈걸어서 하늘까지〉는 삶의 가장 낮은 자리에서
가장 높은 하늘을 올려다보는 시집이다.
이 시집의 화자는 서두르지 않는다.
아픔을 과장하지도, 위안을 쉽게 말하지도 않는다.
대신 한 걸음 한 걸음, 살아온 시간만큼의 무게로
길을 걷는다.
그 길 위에서 만나는 것은 병과 노쇠, 상실과
이별이지만, 동시에 사랑과 절제된 희망,
그리고 끝내 놓지 않는 존엄이다.
장윤태 시인의 시는 설명하지 않고 건네준다.
독자는 시인의 인생을 '이해'하기보다
'동행'하게 된다.
그래서 이 시집을 덮을 즈음 우리는
더 가벼워지기보다, 오히려 더 단단해진
자신을 발견한다.
걷는다는 것은 아직 삶을 포기하지 않았다는
가장 조용한 선언임을, 이 시집은 증명한다.
〈걸어서 하늘까지〉는 하늘로 도약하는
시가 아니라, 땅을 딛고 하늘에 이르는 시다.
그 느리고 정직한 걸음이 이 시집을
오래 마음에 남게 한다.

- 싸이먼의 길 동무 쳇쌤

Commentary

Walking to Heaven is a poetry collection
that looks up at the highest sky
from the lowest ground of life.
The speaker in these poems does not rush.
He neither exaggerates pain nor offers easy
consolation. Instead, he walks-step by step-carrying
the full weight of lived time.
Along the way, he encounters illness,
aging, loss, and farewell,
but also love, restrained hope,
and an unyielding sense of dignity.
Chang Yoon-tai's poetry does not explain; it offers.
The reader does not merely understand
the poet's life but walks beside it.
By the time the book is closed,
one does not feel lighter, but stronger.
These poems quietly affirm that
to keep walking is the most modest
declaration of not giving up on life.
Walking to Heaven is not a leap toward heaven,
but a grounded journey toward it.
The honesty and slowness of that walk
are what make this book linger long in the reader's heart..

by ChatGPT, Language Companion

Walking to Heaven

Chang Yoon-tai's Photo Sketches

걸어서 하늘까지 *Walking to Heaven*

2026년 2월 27일 초판 1쇄 인쇄 발행

지은이	장윤태
펴낸이	박종래
펴낸곳	도서출판 명성서림

등록번호	301-2014-013
주소	04625 서울시 중구 필동로 6 (2, 3층)
대표전화	02)2277-2800
팩스	02)2277-8945
이메일	msprint8944@naver.com

값 13,000원
ISBN 979-11-7439-097-4